Alice in Wonderland

Illustrated by

GREG HILDEBRANDT

From an adaptation by

Lewis Carroll

The Unicorn Publishing House
New Jersey

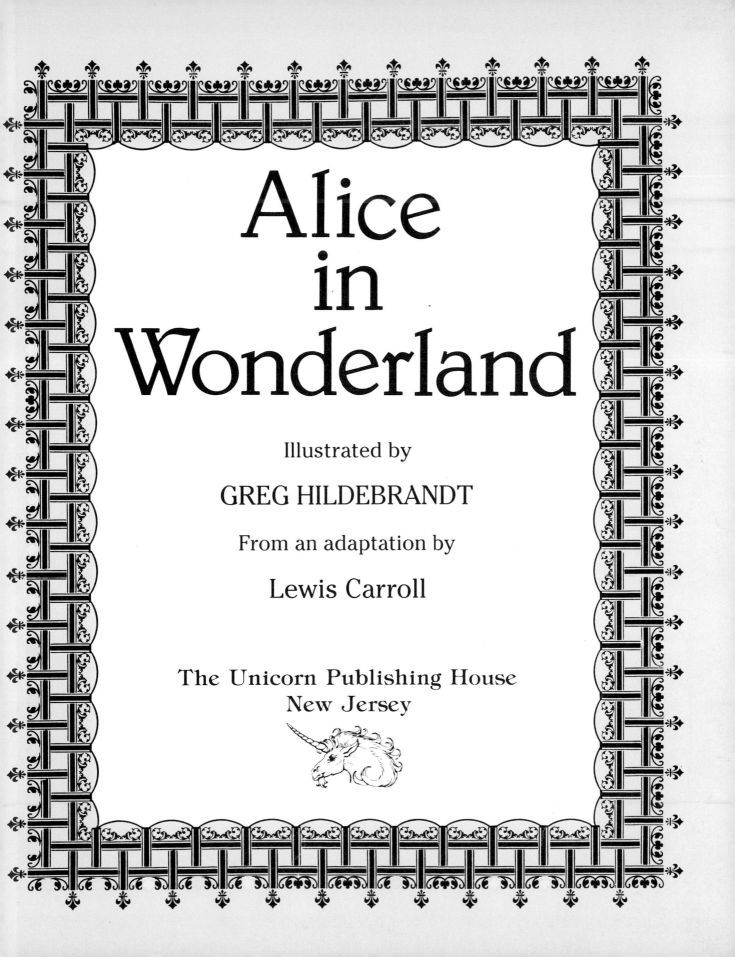

I.
THE WHITE RABBIT.

nce upon a time, there was a little girl called Alice: and she had a very curious dream.
Would you like to hear what it was that she dreamed about?
Well, this was the *first* thing that happened. A White Rabbit came running by, in a great hurry; and, just as it passed Alice, it stopped, and took its watch out of its pocket.

Wasn't *that* a funny thing? Did *you* ever see a Rabbit that had a watch, and a pocket to put it in? Of course, when a Rabbit has a watch, it *must* have a pocket to put it in: it would never do to carry it about in its mouth—and it wants its hands sometimes, to run about with.

"Oh dear, oh dear!" said the Rabbit. "I shall be too late!" What would it be too *late* for, I wonder? Well, you see, it had to go and visit the Duchess: and the Duchess was a very cross old lady: and the Rabbit *knew* she'd be very angry indeed if he kept her waiting. So the poor thing was as frightened as frightened could be (Don't you see how he's trembling? Just shake the book a little, from side to side, and you'll soon see him tremble), because he thought the Duchess would have his head cut off, for a punishment. That was what the Queen of Hearts used to do, when she was angry with people: at least she used to *order* their heads to be cut off, and she always thought it was done, though they never *really* did it.

And so, when the White Rabbit ran away, Alice wanted to see what would happen to it; so she ran after it: and she ran, and she ran, till she tumbled right down the rabbit-hole.

And then she had a very long fall indeed. Down, and down, and down, till she began to wonder if she was going right *through* the World, so as to come out on the other side!

It was just like a very deep well: only there was no water in it. If anybody *really* had such a fall as that, it would kill them, most likely: but you know it doesn't hurt a bit to fall in a *dream*, because, all the time you think you're falling, you really are lying somewhere, safe and sound, and fast asleep!

However, this terrible fall came to an end at last, and down came Alice on a heap of sticks and dry leaves. But she wasn't a bit hurt, and up she jumped, and ran after the Rabbit again.

And so that was the beginning of Alice's curious dream.

II.
HOW ALICE GREW TALL.

And so, after Alice had tumbled down the rabbit-hole, and had run a long long way underground, all of a sudden she found herself in a great hall, with doors all round it.

But all the doors were locked: so, you see, poor Alice couldn't get out of the hall: and that made her very sad.

However, after a little while, she came to a little table, all made of glass, with three legs, and on the table was a little key: and she went round the hall, and tried if she could unlock any of the doors with it.

Poor Alice! The key wouldn't unlock *any* of the doors. But at last she came upon a tiny little door: and oh, how glad she was, when she found the key would fit it!

So she unlocked the tiny little door, and she stooped down and looked through it, and what do you think she saw? Oh, such a beautiful garden! And she did so long to go into it!

But the door was *far* too small. She couldn't squeeze herself through, any more than you could squeeze yourself into a mouse-hole!

So poor little Alice locked up the door, and took the key back to the table again: and *this* time she found quite a new thing on it. It was a little bottle, with a label tied to it, with the words "DRINK ME" on the label.

So she tasted it: and it was *very* nice indeed: so she set to work, and drank it up. And then such a curious thing happened to her! You'll never guess what it was: so I shall have to tell you. She got smaller, and smaller, till at last she was just the size of a little doll!

Then she said to herself "*Now* I'm the right size to get through the little door!" And away she ran. But, when she got there, the door was locked, and the key was on top of the table, and she couldn't reach it! What a pity she had locked up the door again.

Well, the next thing she found was a little cake: and it had the words "EAT ME" marked on it. So of course she set to work and ate it up. And *then* what do you think happened to her? No, you'll never guess! I shall have to tell you again.

She grew, and she grew, and she grew. Taller than she was before! Taller than *any* child! Taller than any grown-up person! Taller, and taller, and taller!

III.
THE POOL OF TEARS.

Perhaps you think Alice must have been very much pleased, when she had eaten the little cake, to find herself growing so tremendously tall? Because of course it would be easy enough, now, to reach the little key off the glass table, and to open the little tiny door.

Well, of course she could do *that:* but what good was it to get the door open, when she couldn't get through? She was worst off than ever! She could just manage, by putting her head down, close to the ground, to look through with one eye! But that was *all* she could do. No wonder the poor tall child sat down and cried as if her heart would break.

So she cried, and she cried. And her tears ran down the middle of the hall, like a deep river. And very soon there was quite a large Pool of Tears, reaching half-way down the hall.

And there she might have stayed, till this very day, if the White Rabbit hadn't happened to come through the hall, on his way to visit the Duchess. He had a pair of white kid gloves in one hand, and a little fan in the other: and he kept muttering to himself "Oh, the Duchess, the Duchess! Oh, *won't* she be savage if I've kept her waiting!"

But he didn't see Alice, you know. So, when she began to say "If you please, Sir—" her voice seemed to come from the top of the hall, because her head was so high up. And the Rabbit was dreadfully frightened: and he dropped the gloves and the fan, and ran away as hard as he could go. Then a *very* curious thing indeed happened. Alice took up the fan, and, lo and behold, she got quite small again, and, all in a minute, she was just about the size of a mouse!

Alice soon found herself in what she thought was a sea, a very salty sea. But it really was a Pool of Tears—all made from *Alice's* tears, you know!

And as Alice swam about, a Mouse happened by, and Alice thought she would have a word or two with him. But the Mouse would have none of it, and began to swim away. Why, you wonder? Well, the reason is, that Alice began talking about cats and dogs: and a Mouse always *hates* talking about cats and dogs!

Suppose you were swimming about, in a Pool of Tears: and suppose somebody began talking to you about lesson-books and bottles of medicine, wouldn't you swim away as hard as you could go?

IV.
THE CAUCUS-RACE.

When Alice and the Mouse had got out of the Pool of Tears, of course they were very wet: and so were a lot of other curious creatures, that had tumbled in as well. There was a Dodo; and a Owl; and a Frog; and several others.

Well, and so they didn't know how in the world they were to get dry again. But the Dodo—who was a very wise bird— told them the right way was to have a Caucus-Race. And what do you think that was?

You don't know? Well, be very attentive, and I shall tell you!

First, you must have a *racecourse*. It ought to be a sort of circle, but it doesn't much matter what shape it is, so long as it goes a good way round, and joins on to itself again.

Then, you must put all the racers on the course, here

and there: it doesn't matter where, so long as you don't crowd them too close together.

Then, you needn't say "One, two, three, and away!" but let them all set off running just when they like, and leave off just when they like.

So all these creatures, Alice and all, went on running round and round, till they were all quite dry again. And then the Dodo said *everybody* had won, and *everybody* must have prizes!

Of course Alice had to give them their prizes. And she had nothing to give them but a few comfits she happened to have in her pocket. And there was just one a-piece, all round. And there was no prize for Alice!

So what do you think they did? Alice had nothing left but her thimble.

"Hand it over here!" said the Dodo.

Then the Dodo took the thimble and handed it back to Alice, and said "We beg your acceptance of this elegant thimble!" And then all the other creatures cheered. What a curious sort of present to give her, don't you think?

V.
BILL, THE LIZARD.

Now I'm going to tell you about Alice's Adventures in the White Rabbit's house.

Do you remember how the Rabbit dropped his gloves and his fan, when he was so frightened at hearing Alice's voice, that seemed to come down from the sky? Well, of course he couldn't go to visit the Duchess *without* his gloves and his fan: so, after a bit, he came back again to look

for them.

By this time the Dodo and all the other curious creatures had gone away, and Alice was wandering about all alone.

So what do you think he did? Actually he thought she was his housemaid, and began ordering her about! "Mary Ann!" he said. "Go home this very minute, and fetch me a pair of gloves and a fan! Quick, now!"

Perhaps he couldn't see very clearly with his pink eyes: for I'm sure Alice doesn't look very like a housemaid, *does* she? However she was a very good-natured little girl: so she wasn't a bit offended, but ran off to the Rabbit's house as quick as she could.

It was lucky she found the door open: for, if she had had to ring, I suppose the *real* Mary Ann would come to open the door: and she would never have let Alice come in. And I'm sure it was very lucky she didn't meet the real Mary Ann, as she trotted upstairs: for I'm afraid she would have taken Alice for a robber!

So at last she found her way into the Rabbit's room: and there was a pair of gloves lying on the table, and she was just going to take them up and go away, when she happened to see a little bottle on the table. And of course it had the words "DRINK ME!" on the label. And of course Alice drank some!

Well, I think that was rather lucky, too: don't you? For, if she *hadn't* drunk any, all this wonderful adventure, that I'm going to tell you about, wouldn't have happened at all. And wouldn't that have been a pity?

You're getting so used to Alice's Adventures, that I daresay you can guess what happened next? If you can't, I'll tell you.

She grew, and she grew, and she grew. And in a very short

time the room was full of *Alice*; just in the same way as a jar is full of jam! There was *Alice* all the way up to the ceiling: and *Alice* in every corner of the room!

The door opened inwards: so of course there wasn't any room to open it: so when the Rabbit got tired of waiting, and came to fetch his gloves for himself, of course he couldn't get in.

So what do you think he did? He sent Bill, the Lizard, up to the roof of the house, and told him to get down the chimney. But Alice happened to have one of her feet in the fire-place: so, when she heard Bill coming down the chimney, she just gave a little tiny kick, and away went Bill, flying up into the sky!

Poor little Bill! How frightened he must have been!

"There goes Bill!" a chorus of voices sounded outside. Then Alice heard the Rabbit say "Catch him, you by the hedge!" then silence, followed by a confusion of voices saying "What happened to you? Tell us all about it!"

"All I know is," began Bill in a feeble, squeaking voice, "something comes at me like a Jack-in-the-box, and up I goes like a sky-rocket!"

"So you did, old fellow, so you did!" said the others.

VI.
THE DEAR LITTLE PUPPY.

Well, while everyone was taking care of Bill, Alice had found some of those little magic cakes, and eaten one. It made her get quite small, directly, so that she could get through the door and out of the White Rabbit's House.

Out in the woods, Alice ran into a little Puppy. Well, it

doesn't look such a very little Puppy, does it? But then, you see, Alice had grown very small indeed: and that's what makes the Puppy look so large.

So it really *was* a little Puppy, you see. And look at the way it's barking at the little stick that Alice is holding out for it! You see, Alice was a *little* afraid of it, all the time, for fear it should run over her. That would have been just about as bad, for her, as it would be for you to be run over by a wagon and four horses.

Alice quickly threw the stick and the little Puppy happily chased after it. Then Alice ran the other way before the Puppy came bounding back, tail wagging, for another toss.

VII.
THE BLUE CATERPILLAR.

Would you like to know what happened to Alice, after she had got away from the Puppy? It was too large an animal, you know, for her to play with. (I don't suppose *you* would much enjoy playing with a young Hippopotamus, would you? You would always be expecting to be crushed as flat as a pancake under its great heavy feet!) So Alice was very glad to run away, while it wasn't looking.

Well, she wandered up and down, and didn't know what in the world to do, to make herself grow up to her right size again.

Of course she knew that she had to eat or drink *something*: that was the regular rule, you know: but she couldn't guess *what* thing.

However, she soon came to a great mushroom, that was so tall that she could barely see over it. And what do

you think she saw? Something that I'm sure you never talked to, in all your life!

It was a large Blue Caterpillar. The caterpillar was sitting on top, quietly smoking a long hookah, and taking not the smallest notice of Alice or of anything else.

The Caterpillar and Alice looked at each other for some time in silence: at last the Caterpillar took the hookah out of its mouth, and spoke to Alice with a slow, sleepy voice.

And what did Alice and the Caterpillar talk about, I wonder?

Well, Alice told it how very confusing it was, being first one size and then another.

And the Caterpillar asked her if she liked the size she was, just then.

And Alice said she would like to be just a little bit larger—three inches was such a *wretched* height to be! (By the way, the Caterpillar didn't care for her dislike for the size of three inches: for the Caterpillar, you see, was just exactly three inches long, and he thought three inches to be the perfect size indeed, anyway you measure it.)

And the Caterpillar told her one side of the mushroom would make her grow *taller*, and the other side would make her grow *shorter*. Then the Caterpillar yawned once or twice, shook itself, and climbing off the mushroom, crawled away into the grass.

Alice remained looking thoughtfully at the mushroom for a minute, trying to make out which were the two sides of it; and, as it was perfectly round, she found this a very difficult question. But, finally, Alice took two little bits of it with her to nibble, and managed to make herself quite a nice comfortable height, before she went on to visit the Duchess.

VIII.
THE PIG-BABY.

Would you like to hear about Alice's visit to the Duchess? It was a very interesting visit indeed, I can assure you.

Of course she knocked at the door to begin with—but nobody came—so she had to open it for herself.

The door led right into the kitchen, you see. The Duchess sat in the middle of the room, nursing the Baby. The Baby was howling. The soup was boiling. The Cook was stirring the soup, sometimes, and throwing dishes at the Duchess, othertimes.

The Duchess had on a beautiful cap and gown, but I'm afraid her face was, you might say, far from beautiful.

The Baby—well, I daresay you've seen several nicer babies than that: and more good-tempered ones, too. And the Cook—well, you may have seen nicer cooks, too, once or twice.

Now, the Duchess was very rude to Alice. And no wonder. Why, she even called her own *Baby* "Pig!" And it *wasn't* a Pig, was it? And she ordered the Cook to chop off Alice's head: though of course the Cook didn't do it; but instead, threw another dish at the Duchess. And at last the Duchess turned to Alice, and threw the Baby at her! So Alice caught the Baby, and took it away with her: and I think that was about the best thing she could do.

So she wandered away, through the wood, carrying the ugly little thing with her. And a great job it was to keep hold of it, it wriggled about so. But at last she found out that the proper way was, to keep tight hold of its left foot and its right ear.

But don't *you* try to hold on to a Baby like that! There are not many babies that like being held in that way!

Well, and so the Baby kept grunting, and grunting, so that Alice had to say to it, quite seriously, "If you're going to turn into a *Pig*, my dear, I'll have nothing more to do with you. Mind now!"

And at last she looked down into its face, and what do you think had happened to it?

It turned into a little Pig!

So Alice put it down, and let it trot away into the wood. And she said to herself "It was a *very* ugly Baby: but it makes rather a handsome Pig, I think."

IX.
THE CHESHIRE-CAT.

All alone, all alone! Poor Alice! No Baby, not even a Pig to keep her company!

So you may be sure she was very glad indeed, when she saw the Cheshire-Cat, perched up in a tree, over her head.

The Cat has a very nice smile, no doubt: but just look what a lot of teeth it's got! Isn't Alice just a *little* shy of it?

Well, yes, a little. But then, it couldn't help having teeth, you know: and it could have helped smiling, supposing it had been cross. So, on the whole, she was *glad*.

"Cheshire Puss!" said Alice. (Wasn't that a pretty name for a Cat?) "Would you tell me which way I ought to go from here?"

And so the Cheshire-Cat told her which way she ought to go, if she wanted to visit the Hatter, and which way to go, to visit the March Hare. "They're both mad!" said the Cat.

And then the Cat vanished away, just like the flame of a candle when it goes out!

So Alice set off, to visit the March Hare. And as she went along, there was the Cat again! And she told it she didn't *like* it coming and going so quickly.

So this time the Cat vanished quite slowly, beginning with the tail, and ending with the grin. Wasn't that a curious thing, a Grin without any Cat?

X.
THE MAD TEA-PARTY.

Alice left the Cheshire-Cat, and went off to see the March Hare and the Hatter, as the Cheshire-Cat had advised her: and she found them having tea under a great tree, with a Dormouse sitting between them.

There were only those three at the table, but there were quantities of tea-cups set all along it. You can't see all the table, you know, so you'll just have to take my word about the tea-cups.

There was a *nice* red arm-chair at the end of the table, that looked as if it was just meant for Alice, big and roomy, you see, so she went and sat down in it. Then she had quite a long talk with the March Hare and the Hatter. The Dormouse didn't say much. You see it was fast asleep generally, and it only just woke up for a moment, now and then.

As long as it was asleep, it was very useful to the March Hare and the Hatter, because it had a nice round soft head, just like a pillow: so they could put their elbows on it, and lean across it, and talk to each other quite comfortably. You wouldn't like people to use your head for a pillow, would

you? But if you were fast asleep, like the Dormouse, you wouldn't feel it: so I suppose you wouldn't care about it.

I'm afraid they gave Alice *very* little to eat and drink. However, after a bit, she helped herself to some tea and bread-and-butter. But nobody seemed to have a plate except the Hatter. I believe the March Hare must have had one as well: because, when they all moved one place on (that was the rule at this curious tea-party), and Alice had to go into the place of the March Hare, the Dormouse made a ruckus and tipped the milk-jug into the plate: at which time the Hatter and March Hare grabbed him up and began *stuffing* him into the tea-pot.

Alice didn't care a bit for their behavior (of course, she didn't expect anything less from a mad tea-party) but nonetheless, she decided it was high time to leave.

XI.
THE QUEEN'S GARDEN.

Alice managed at last to get quite small, nibbling a bit here and there at the pieces of mushroom she still had left: so that she could go through the little door. Do you remember the little door? The one that led into the beautiful garden? I thought you might have forgotten, since Alice has been so many places since then.

Well, I suppose she was about as tall as a mouse, if it stood on its hind-legs: so of course the garden was *very* tiny indeed, with a *very* tiny rose-tree in the corner. And around the tiny rose-tree were tiny little gardeners.

What funny little men they were! But were they men, do you think? I think they must be live cards, with just a head,

and arms, and legs, so as to *look* like little men. And what had they been doing with that red paint, you might ask? Well, you see, this is what they told Alice: The Queen of Hearts wanted to have a *red* rose-tree just in that corner: and these poor little gardeners had made a great mistake, and had put in a *white* one instead: and they were so frightened about it, because the Queen was sure to be angry, and then she would order all their heads to be cut off.

She was a dreadfully savage Queen, and that was the way she always did, when she was angry with people. "Off with *their* heads!" They didn't really cut their heads off, you know: because nobody ever obeyed her: but that was what she always said.

Now can't you guess what the poor little gardeners were trying to do? They were trying to paint the roses red, and were in a great hurry to get it done before the Queen arrived. They worked away, and worked away, knowing full well if they didn't finish in time it would be "Off with *their* heads! Off with *their* heads!"

Well, as you can see, they didn't finish in time! The Queen arrived and was furious! She cried "Off with *their* heads!" and the guards carried them away. But, really, the guards let them go when the Queen wasn't looking.

"Are their heads off?" shouted the Queen.

"Their heads are gone, if it please your Majesty!" the guards shouted in reply

But what about Alice? Well, that's a different story altogether.

"Can you play Croquet?" the Queen asked.

"Yes!" Alice shouted.

"Come on, then!" roared the Queen.

XII.
THE LOBSTER-QUADRILLE.

Did you ever play at Croquet? There are large wooden balls, painted with different colors, that you have to roll about; and arches of wire, that you have to send them through; and great wooden mallets, with long handles, to knock the balls about with.

Now look at the picture, and you'll see that Alice has been playing a Game of Croquet. But how *could* she play, with that great pink what's-its-name in her arms? Why, how could she hold the mallet?

Well, that great pink what's-its-name (of course, its *real* name is "a Flamingo") is the mallet! In this Croquet-Game, the balls were live *Hedge-hogs*—you know a hedge-hog can roll itself up into a ball—and the mallets were live *Flamingos*! But Alice really didn't get a chance to play Croquet: because everytime she tried to hit a hedge-hog, the tiny creatures would move, and everytime she tried to swing the Flamingo, it would bend its neck. The Flamingo would look straight into Alice's face, and it looked so funny, that Alice just couldn't help but laugh.

After the game, the Queen took Alice away to meet two very odd creatures. The Queen took Alice to see the Gryphon and the Mock Turtle.

You don't know what a Gryphon is? Well, indeed! Then I shall tell you. A Gryphon is a creature that is half-bird, half-lion. A fierce looking creature, I admit, but all in all, it is really very gentle.

And what of the Mock Turtle? Well, its turtle shell body always trembles, and its calf eyes are always crying (you

see, the Mock Turtle has the body of a turtle and the head of a calf). Why? No one ever asked. I suppose you would have to ask the Mock Turtle yourself.

And they danced for Alice. They danced a *Lobster-Quadrille* and sang rhymes, too. So if you ever meet a Gryphon and a Mock Turtle, I daresay they'll dance and sing for you, if you ask them nicely. Only don't let them come *too* close, or they'll be treading on your toes.

XIII.
WHO STOLE THE TARTS?

Did you ever hear how the Queen of Hearts made some tarts? And can you tell me what became of them?

"Why, of *course* I can! Doesn't the song tell all about it?

> The Queen of Hearts, she made some tarts;
>   All on a summer day;
> The Knave of Hearts, he stole those tarts,
>   And took them quite away!"

Well, yes, the *Song* says so. But it would never do to punish the poor Knave, just because there was a *Song* about him. They had to take him prisoner, and put chains on his wrists, and bring him before the King of Hearts, so that there might be a regular trial. And a grand thing a trial is, when the Judge is a King!

The King is very grand, isn't he? But he doesn't look very happy. I think that big crown, on top of his wig, must be *very* heavy and uncomfortable. But he had to wear them both, you see, so that people might know he was a Judge *and*

a King.

And doesn't the Queen look cross? She can see the dish of tarts on the table, that she had taken such trouble to make. And she can see the bad Knave (do you see the chains hanging from his wrists?) that stole them away from her: so I don't think it's any wonder if she does feel a *little* cross.

The White Rabbit is standing near the King, reading out the Song, to tell everybody what a bad Knave he is: and the Jury, as you see, is just a bit odd, but nonetheless, they have to settle whether he's "guilty" or "not guilty."

One of the witnesses to be called was the Mad Hatter, who was so nervous, that he showed up without his shoes. And as the King questioned him, the Hatter shook so, and even bit a piece out of his tea-cup. And all through the trial the Queen cried "Off with *his* head! *Their* heads! *All* heads!"

After several witnesses appeared before the King, none of whom shed any light on who stole the tarts, or anything else for that matter, a surprising thing happened— Alice was called as a witness.

But *Alice* hadn't seen the Queen make the tarts: and she hadn't seen the Knave take the tarts: and, in fact, she didn't know anything about it: so why in the world they wanted her to be a witness, I'm sure I can't tell you!

Anyhow, they did want her. And the White Rabbit blew his big trumpet, and shouted out "Alice!" And so Alice jumped up in a great hurry. And then—

And then what do you think happened? Why, her skirt caught against the Jury-box, and tipped it over, and all the poor Jurors came tumbling out of it!

Alice gently picked all up again, very carefully, and helped return them to their Jury-box.

XIV.
THE SHOWER OF CARDS.

Oh dear, what would happen next?

Well, I'll tell you all about it, as well I can. The way the trial ended was this. The King wanted the Jury to settle whether the Knave of Hearts was *guilty* or *not guilty*—that means that they were to settle whether he had stolen the Tarts, or if somebody else had taken them. But the wicked Queen wanted to have his *punishment* settled, first of all. That wasn't at all fair, was it? Because, you know, supposing he never took the Tarts, then of course he oughtn't to be punished. Would you like to be punished for something you hadn't done?

So Alice said "Stuff and nonsense!"

So the Queen said "Off with *her* head!" (Just as she always said, when she was angry.)

So Alice said "Who cares for *you*? You're nothing but a pack of cards!"

So they were all very angry, and flew up into the air, and came tumbling down again, all over Alice, just like a shower of rain.

And I think you'll *never* guess what happened next. The next thing was, Alice woke up out of her curious dream. And she found that the cards were only some leaves off the tree, that the wind had blown down upon her face.

Wouldn't it be a nice thing to have a curious dream, just like Alice?

The best plan is this. First lie down under a tree, and wait till a White Rabbit runs by, with a watch in his hand: then shut your eyes, and pretend to be little Alice.

For over a decade, Unicorn has been
publishing richly illustrated editions of classic
and contemporary works for children and adults.
To continue this tradition,
WE WOULD LIKE TO KNOW WHAT YOU THINK.

If you would like to send us your suggestions or
obtain a list of our current titles, please write to:
THE UNICORN PUBLISHING HOUSE, INC.
P.O. Box 377
Morris Plains, New Jersey, USA 07950
ATT: Dept CLP

❖❖❖❖❖❖❖